PHONICS

So Scary!

Practising long vowel phonemes,
trisyllabic words and tricky words

First published in 2007 by
Franklin Watts
338 Euston Road
London
NW1 3BH

Franklin Watts Australia
Level 17/207 Kent Street
Sydney
NSW 2000

A CIP catalogue record for this book is available
from the British Library.

ISBN: 978 0 7496 7286 7 (hbk)
ISBN: 978 0 7496 7324 6 (pbk)

Series Editor: Jackie Hamley
Series Advisors: Dr Barrie Wade, Dr Hilary Minns
Series Designer: Peter Scoulding

Printed in China

Franklin Watts is a division of
Hachette Children's Books.

PHONICS

So Scary!

by
Anne Adeney

Illustrated by
Gwyneth Williamson

W

FRANKLIN WATTS

LONDON•SYDNEY

Anne Adeney
"Most people are scared of something. What would be the scariest thing for you to find?"

Gwyneth Williamson
"I really, really, really HATE black-hairy-long-leggy SPIDERS! They're so scary!"

Paul was a kind and helpful
knight. He would stalk
and trap scary giants.

One day, a messenger came. Paul put down his bread and meat.

Hurry to my garden right away. There is such a scary thing here! You must free me from it.

From Lady June

Paul rode his brown horse
over the mountain.

He saw Lady June in her fine, blue gown.

Suddenly, Paul saw a very scary shadow. He took out his knife. Smoke was all around him.

Suddenly, he saw a red
and yellow flash.

12

Paul saw the knife in his
hand begin to melt.

Would the thing roast him?

Would it eat him?

It was so scary that his knees felt like jelly.

But he must make
Lady June safe.

Paul got his rope
over the thing's
head and wings.

19

Lady June began to cry out:
"You mean knight! Don't
do that to my pet!"

Lady June began to cuddle
her scary pet.

"Silly knight! This is Green Tail!
The *scary* thing is over there!"

Paul found the scary thing on a jug in the middle of a table.

It had eight black, hairy legs,
but it was quite little.

Soon, Paul was lifting it up
with a gentle hand.

28

He took it far away from Lady
June and put it on a tree.

Now, Paul, Lady June and Green
Tail are all happy again.

Notes for parents and teachers

READING CORNER PHONICS has been structured to provide maximum support for children learning to read through synthetic phonics. The stories are designed for independent reading but may also be used by adults for sharing with young children.

The teaching of early reading through synthetic phonics focuses on the 44 sounds in the English language, and how these sounds correspond to their written form in the 26 letters of the alphabet. Carefully controlled vocabulary makes these books accessible for children at different stages of phonics teaching, progressing from simple CVC (consonant-vowel-consonant) words such as "top" (t-o-p) to trisyllabic words such as "messenger" (mess-en-ger). READING CORNER PHONICS allows children to read words in context, and also provides visual clues and repetition to further support their reading. These books will help develop the all important confidence in the new reader, and encourage a love of reading that will last a lifetime!

If you are reading this book with a child, here are a few tips:

1. Talk about the story before you start reading. Look at the cover and the title. What might the story be about? Why might the child like it?

2. Encourage the child to reread the story, and to retell the story in their own words, using the illustrations to remind them what has happened.

3. Discuss the story and see if the child can relate it to their own experience, or perhaps compare it to another story they know.

4. Give praise! Small mistakes need not always be corrected. If a child is stuck on a word, ask them to try and sound it out and then blend it together again, or model this yourself. For example "wish" w-i-sh "wish".

READING CORNER PHONICS covers two grades of synthetic phonics teaching, with three levels at each grade. Each level has a certain number of words per story, indicated by the number of bars on the spine of the book:

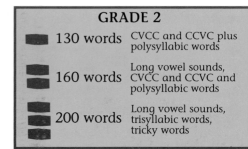

GRADE 1	
50 words	CVC words with short vowel sounds
70 words	CVC words plus sounds of more than one letter
100 words	Sounds of more than one letter, simple polysyllabic words

GRADE 2	
130 words	CVCC and CCVC plus polysyllabic words
160 words	Long vowel sounds, CVCC and CCVC and polysyllabic words
200 words	Long vowel sounds, trisyllabic words, tricky words